PARTHENOGENESIS

&

PLAGUE
IN THE IMPERIAL CITY

Peter Valente

Foreword by Murat Nemet-Nejat

SPUYTEN DUYVIL
NEW YORK CITY

©2017 Peter Valente
ISBN 978-1-944682-60-6

Library of Congress Cataloging-In-Publication data applied for.

Transformations in Peter Valente's Imperial Cities
Murat Nemet-Nejat

In Peter Valente's extraordinary science fiction diptych science and magic meet, the future is prologue to the past, and what is between them is absolute chaos that raises its head as a mysterious disease, a plague out of Oedipus's Thebes injected by a computer virus, full of assassins and astral travel.

Oedipus must gouge his eyes—the state becoming invisible to him—to heal it. Valente's Imperial City must succumb to the plague to be healed in a new eon of the self.

Valente's ever elusive, ever shape shifting narrator says, "the art of invisibility is a necessary requirement for rebellion—the spirit jumping to its other invisible self that follows the person everywhere like a shadow cast by a sun shining inside the brain."

Shadows are dispersed everywhere in the Imperial City but still the rhythm of another heartbeat conducts them—leading to an alternate double across psychocosmic space.

That heart beat—dark, violent, visionary—is the driving narrative of Valente's work. The reader must approach it at his or her own peril: "Magic draws from the forbidden… the first magical act is becoming aware that I AM a self…distinct from others who carry the same social role…Destroy what is destroying you/us…the dance is Shiva… we are the gods…"

The Achilles' heel of every utopian re-casting is discovered:

"The double is looking at the sky. There remains in her a vague sense of her former self. All the digital reprogramming could not eradicate it. This causes the double to hallucinate where her former self would see clearly. The digital perception is flawed and causes an upheaval in the system. The double cannot fully replicate the original. As the body approaches the state of total replication the transfer from 0 to infinity must occur on the subatomic level. It is a race towards the infinite that is doomed. There is no reaching this terminal state. It is a theoretical convention. And so Jezebel wanders the city as a ghost.

A single leaf, as if magnetized, in defiance of gravity, remains still in the negative air.

The traveller vanishes   his disappearance leaves a rupture in space-time.

He enters the invisible

A fierce wind blows in the desert

A window opens in the space-time continuum.

The EYE closes. What was formerly a city is now a vast desert. A hole in space is now closed. The elapsed time erased."

Parthenogenesis

June, 1969

What follows is my attempt to relate the very strange circumstances surrounding my transformation into a hermaphroditic god. I am doing this for myself and also for a certain painter friend of mine. I will simply call myself "the traveller" in order not to arouse suspicion among those who knew me in what I now understand was my previous incarnation. I had come to assassinate the Commander but my life took an extraordinary turn when, as a result, I encountered the people of the invisible world. But I am saying too much already. Let the text speak for itself.

In recreating the events I have used original documents whenever available but more often I simply relied on the memory of what I saw. I have tried to give the reader a sense of what it was to experience that place. I was an unwilling participant in a world saturated with information, a ceaseless barrage of signs that converged, in my case, toward a frightening and marvelous truth.

From The Traveller's Notebook
November 23, 3:24 pm

Ready to board flight in an hour. Nervous. Not sure this is the right thing to do. My wife begged me not to go. Sick to my stomach. What will happen if I don't manage to gain access to the Commander's secret chambers? I've studied all the documents and newspaper clippings, read all the required books. Nothing seems to ease my nerves. Something doesn't add up. I feel that I am heading straight into the mouth of hell.

Report 1

It is not merely noise the traveller hears continuing to turn the corner of the empty street arrived at 10:35 pm in this place surrounded by desert something wrong he could feel it in the air something very wrong with the strangers he meets surviving ending in arranged holes of intellectual depth they carry guns to remote outposts better weapons lead to better and better weapons find tins of junk they carry on their backs bumping against one another not revealing anything others milling around in the grass under the hot sun there are restless forces at work here that make the techniques effective they expand outward seeking territories embedded crudely in the geography with outdated maps old fashioned tools roads that lead nowhere in particular The Commander refuses to talk with his inferiors a new beginning he says is imminent measures modifies habits of language and behavior toward an ideal of knowledge a glowing virus spreads uncontrollably among the populace there is no work but ruthless investments organized behind the camps accelerating production unable to stop generating aesthetic pleasure as entertainment cluttered with illusions the world came crashing down once on a screen without depth in some remote foreign coast near the oil spills livestock infected the water unfit to drink they tilt their bodies towards the black fur of some prehistoric god at dawn they are moved by ecstatic prayer looking far down inside the earth or above for god knows what he thinks they are trained to see what is not there a voice from the imaginary telephone wired to the brain they obey commands keep to themselves hardly speak of anything but practical matters he feels an odd sensation as he closes his lids here under a different name he clutches a few last dead leaves half buried in mud near the financial district.

From The Traveller's Notebook
November 26, 11:37 PM

Been here three days. Eaten very little. No one around. Seems to be some kind of religious holiday. Can't make heads or tails of the signs posted throughout the city. Hermetic symbols or just plain scribble. Don't know what the people do here but they seem afraid of something. Don't know what. Imagine I'll find out. I wasn't born an assassin. How did I get into this? Sure, they pay well but.... that couldn't be the only reason....

Telepathic Transmission 1

Society, despite the charming and misinformed view of early popular anthropology, predates humanity. The self is a recent enough invention that there are still societies which have little or no self-definition in their members. Rather, the individual is defined almost entirely by *role*.

Report 2

The traveller enters the Circle of Hell where he sees an order of cool machines buzzing in every corner new scents mirrors magic pills men and women upstairs downstairs in partitioned rooms or in vestibules behind the main door the smell of sperm and sodomy alcohol and urine the sound of chains swinging the crack of whips coughs screams the air moist with human secretions writhing personalities bodies indistinct from one another form a singular entity of meat and bone in ecstasy of violet light and harsh industry fingers full of energy on the keys behind the scenes programming the series of pleasures read as omens on the walls of the city's scribbled geometries hermetic symbols new age proclamations while the pipes freeze at the border and cold sets in breathing is difficult beyond a certain point sickness lurking around the corner in the distance you can see the glare of the Paradise hotel.

THE COMMANDER'S SECRET CHAMBERS:

What's his name?   We don't know.   Why is he here?   We're not sure.
We've sent word to our people.   Something should turn up.   These foreigners think they can get away with anything.   They are ignorant scum.
Parasitic insects.
But there are so many of them.   We have to use them as we can.

WHO THE FUCK IS HE?

This is a city completely altered by advances in bioengineering. There are two distinct classes in the order of bodies. The entire ruling class is both human and bionic. The Commander's arms and legs have been rewired and digitized. This is also the case with his brain. A mini computer has been installed to allow for greater mnemonic capabilities and tactical acumen. This is also the case with secret agents and chiefs of staff. It is a very expensive procedure. Every year, with every advance in science, the upper classes replace a part of the body. The goal is to erase the human and to create fully functional androids. The populace is simply human, flesh and bone, and thus at a significant disadvantage. Subject to age and decay.

The challenge to science, of course, is the human heart. It cannot be replicated with accuracy.

Telepathic Transmission 2

This city is hopeless. Even its garbage is clean, its traffic lubricated, its movement pacified.

From The Traveller's Notebook
December 10, 6:42 am

The C.O.H OK. Got a bit too drunk. Reminds me of some places back in New York in the 90's. Got word someone could help me there. Someone with access to the Commander's secret rooms. False lead. Plain bullshit, really. Can't trust anyone in this place.

Jezebel looks up at the sky.   Her arms upraised make the sign of the beetle god.

The traveller calls his wife

Honey?.....Claire? .....can you hear me?......Paul?....no, no names....it's a bad connection.....hello?....hello?....How are you doing?....hello?....You sound very distant....Claire? There's too much interference......Claire?....Claire?...yes I'm here.... I'm here, darling...I just wanted to...Claire?....hello?.... hello?.....hello? ………………………………………………..

Telepathic Transmission 3

What communication does in a role-based interchange is reinforce the group identity of the participants.

Telepathic Transmission 4

Negotiation unfruitful. Tension mounts.

Is he out of his fucking mind? In broad daylight.   Send a brief to Martin.

Martin is just waking up when he hears his cell ring. Hello? Get your ass down here………..The rest is noise. 15 minutes later he realizes what he must do. Gets up lights a cigarette brews coffee sits down in the kitchen thinks another one on the list another poor sap on the Commander's shit list. Martin was a homeless drug addict before he hooked up with the Commander through a prostitute at the CIRCLE OF HELL. He was cleaned up given a new suit trained built up through the "confidence technique." He turned into a raging machine. He's what they call the "charmer" whose function is to warn foreigners that they are not welcome a right hook to the jaw not too much blood Above him are the "assassins" and above them the "evacuation squad."

Telepathic Transmission 5

STATE OF THE UNION

Constitutional psychopathic states:

1. Sexual psychopathology 93%
2. Drug addiction 42%
3. Psychoneurosis, hysteria 60%
4. Schizophrenia 19%

A Brief From The Commander's Secret Chambers

One of the benefits of using clones is that the genetic bio-information will be automatically stored. It will have the subject's walk, speech, mannerisms, even bowel movements.

Report 3

The sovereign body affects essential interests like watching tv programs at night alone you question family death love it's a cartwheel life of distraction everywhere you go so you withdraw opposition face people maintain healthy interests to the tone of administration dynamics crude growth of feeling in the robot swarm each morning.

Telepathic Transmission 6

Western man may be said to have been undergoing a massive sensory anesthesia called bureaucratic rationalization at least since the industrial revolution.

The Commander Speaks To His Chief Of Staff

It's necessary these days. All those stupid little soldiers have a hard on for big daddy. You have to give them the opportunity to ejaculate, otherwise they'll get pimples and they'll go home crying like babies to their mommies. It's not right to disappoint young people.

Telepathic Transmission 7

The Greek word for icon means "sacred image." The function of the icon is to objectify belief and to pacify the believer. Anything can be a sacred image. Art in the twentieth century has shown us this. But in order to be effective it must be specific: a smartphone, lady gaga, the image of ben franklin on a crumpled 100 dollar bill, an erect penis, the drug ecstasy, spring fashions. You get the idea.

From The Traveller's Notebook
December 21, 7:02 am

He came out of nowhere. One of the Commander's agents I think. Or some local punk. Wrong street. Wrong time of night. It gets so dark around here you can barely see anything at night. Got to heal this cut on my forehead before I can leave this room. The Paradise Hotel. What a dump. In any case, don't want to attract attention. Wonder how much they know already.

While going through footage of the Commander's torture chambers, the revolutionaries discover him having sex with children and crippled adults.

The films are shipped overseas.

On January 2 at 4:16 pm the traveller heard someone slipping a piece of paper under his door. On the paper was written:

I INVOKE THE SIGN OF THE AVENGING ANGEL

At 4:30pm the same day he heard an explosion. He looked outside his window and could see smoke in the far distance. The Paradise Hotel was located in a remote area near the border. For him to have heard anything at all meant the devastation must have been massive. He looked down at the piece of paper and read. Could there be some connection?

A bomb detonates near the train station. No one is killed. But hundreds of commuters are stranded. After a few hours, screams can be heard from the seething mass. There is a smell of body odor and piss in the air. Accompanied by rabid fear.

Report 5

To control the future streaming in digital don't ask questions open your fortifications distribute shrink-wrapped packages in secret monthly at special rates set by the Commander funny it seems data can translate feeling and keep it real and exciting feeding the topic under analysis it works you're happy a total rush in the mind uploading realities getting closer to planned intercourse discussing precious method where the ambient noise of resistance becomes a nuisance.

From The Traveller's Notebook
Jan 4, 5:13 pm

A knock at my door. A chill of fear rises up in me. No one comes to the Paradise for no reason. No one is supposed to know that I am here. Maybe it is a vagrant worker displaced as a result of the bomb scare. But here? A moment of silence. Then a knock a pause then another. Then 3 more in rapid succession. The visitor seems impatient. I walk towards the door, firmly clutch the knob, pause for a moment, brace myself, then open the door. I could not believe what I saw then…..

That's right I know who you are. How? Forget "how." I know why you're here. But….No questions. I can help you. Do you smoke? I light her cigarette. The fact is you're not safe here and I can help you. This is what you must do. Here take this card. See the number scrawled on the back? Call that number. You'll hear a voice on the other end. Don't ask any questions. Don't ask for names. They won't ask for yours. They will give you directions. Follow them. They'll lead to our headquarters. There you'll learn the truth about this place.

From The Traveller's Notebook, Jan 6, 7:29am

She said her name was Jezebel. My luck! She was wearing red leather pants and a transparent black lace top. She wore dark glasses that she never took off. Her head was shaved. On the middle finger of her left hand was a ring inscribed with a magical symbol. I think it was the eye of Horus. But I couldn't be sure. Magic isn't my thing. In any case she radiated a certain unusual energy. Her voice was as deep as a man's. Even her gestures, the way she manipulated her cigarette and shifted in her seat, was alternately masculine and feminine. Indeed there was something about her that was essentially androgynous.

I called the number and followed her directions. I was led to an obscure part of town behind the military posts past a few trees down a winding path toward a flight of stairs to a door which led to a room whose red glare was at once disorienting and supremely sensuous.

Report 6

Disease with a touch of grace out here in these wastelands the habit of vision changes forever O what splendor everlasting physical torment despite warlike success not enough profit yet radiant energies of drone craft alight over heavily populated areas another motto broadcast over the dead air and plastered on a screen troops continue carelessly into the future knowing actions right but execution returns false face of Capital and failing popularity look ahead and see signs of ice the essential farce in every report shredded burned and forgotten for a while there is dummy rage and then the quick turnaround.

Telepathic Transmission 8

In ten seconds, how many synonyms can you think of for the word "power"?

From The Traveller's Notebook
Jan 15, 8:43am

I secretly recorded some of what I heard at the home of the People of the Phoenix. They are the sole revolutionary element in this decaying city. They occasionally release what they call " reports" on their website which is encrypted and cannot be hacked. The "telepathic transmissions" are spray painted on walls throughout the city. In this way they communicate their ideas to the people.

I've begun transcribing parts of the recording: **Magic draws from the forbidden…hence the "dark" or "black magic"…its elements have never been approved by society at large…the first magical act is becoming aware that I AM a self…distinct from others who carry the same social role…Destroy what is destroying you/us…the dance is Shiva…we are the gods…**

The rest of the meeting was concerned with practical techniques of revolutionary action. They believe that with the aim of religion and the method of science they can succeed in overthrowing the dominant regime. They said that I was one of them and they have tracked my movements since I arrived here. Much later I realized that these "reports" were, among other things, a kind of history of my own life on the magical plane.

I was sworn to secrecy. They said they would contact me when they needed me.

Report 7

The Valley of introspection remains cut off to enforce the rules of ceaseless repetition the people below the poverty line wait for something to happen they arrive at an aggressive solution and remain dissatisfied when calm returns.

On January 19, the traveller has a dream in which he sees Jezebel in front of a tall building in the financial district. He realizes that the Commander is inside. She is holding up a sign on which is written:

THE CIRCLE IS DRAWN AND THE LAUGHING GOD INVOKED

Suddenly he is in a room and the Commander is in front of him having sex with a young male hustler. The Commander cannot see him.

The Commander feels an uncontrollable desire to defecate. "Get the fuck off me you stupid punk"

The traveller awakes laughing.

Telepathic Transmission 9

They preached that social conditions were under a divine plan, not capable of being understood by man, and that fatalism and resignation were the proper response.

Report 8

Nervous laughter of children at the crowded stations The Commander announces various unsung ideas of the past messianic effulgence to salvage vitality there is a nagging sense of world apocalypse by fire these are unspeakable wars you sleep dream of fabled utopias scenes from old movies iconic figures lodged in the collective unconscious while the stream goes dry blood runs along the outer banks the numerous dead float in the river the stench is unbearable you cannot believe what is happening to you Eating ice for breakfast the Commander comprehends new forms of energy That same lucid night men are killed or wounded in the trenches all seems natural clean and ready to go.

Report 9

Men killed in the line of duty a wilderness of lines keeping things even suppressing an urge to look back and examine the documents in full maintaining combat sorrow silence.

Martin returns home after the job feeling depressed. He lies down in bed. Lights a cigarette. Looks up at the dirty cracked ceiling. He can hear a pounding next door. Nothing else. Just someone banging on something. He's been holed up in the Paradise for six months. He turns on the tv... **click**

At my age I must watch my figure... **click**

Call toll free... **click**

I'm from the government I'm here to help you... **click**

A revolutionary new method of infant feeding... **click**

Barbie and Tommy the real story... **click**

Conspiracies Unlimited... **click**

Get your start up package for a small fee of $399... **click**

He shuts if off. He hears the banging sound again. It seems to have grown louder.

When Martin awakes the next morning he decides to take off from work. The Commander will be pissed but he doesn't give a shit. Fuck this life. Fuck what I've become. Day after day going nowhere fast. I'm just the Commander's slave boy. He cleaned me up for what? So I'd rot inside while displaying my white teeth and bashing in those of some poor sap just for being a foreigner. Just for being different. Better to sign off and make a permanent escape.

Report 10

The traveller feels someone watching him too vivid eyes across the street they may be those of the Commander's agents he is driving at night moving pacing himself inside a series of tunnels beyond the logical horizon he feels something is missing despite elaborate schemes scraps of thinking moving pacing himself inside a vacuum until he sees the lights go out the billboards flashing ahead moving to the next stop night air follows him he sees large machines weeds stones along the strip of highway he sees the military posts machines weeds stones there are men at war there is a constant buzzing in his ears somewhere the wheel the stars on the floor block out the moon years of polishing the fragments of writing dulled to an illegible scrawl.

FROM THE TRAVELLER'S NOTEBOOK
JAN 20, 3:19 AM

uninspired spiritual life

Report 11

Looking into a cloud of dust the Traveller sees trees in darkness bits of himself at the end of the line an horizon of empty water listening seeing hearing a picture of rage the repetitious dirge different meanings on the opinion polls along the way useless information for crash test dummies directly out the mouth then gone perhaps a realist view an instant observing the space before you photograph slogan monument those same skills a valuable commodity that has burned away the obscure term in this century of knowledge you turn inward beneath an odor of decay an endless loop of communication on line.

Telepathic Transmission 10

Each year top physicists, linguists, economists, leaders of state, the Commander himself, decide what portion of the Great Secret to release to the public.[1]

---

[1] Excerpt from a rare copy of an underground newspaper thought to be destroyed.

Report 12

The Traveller in darkness standing alone unthinking crushed by vice in unbroken sunlight wearing a mask he stands in fear his ideas fail the sublime gesture.

From The Traveller's Notebook
Feb. 12, 6:39am

I am keeping this notebook as a record of my experiences in this city. If it should be found out why I am here I will be killed. This record allows me to feel that I exist. Without it I could lose myself in this place.

These are a deeply religious people. They worship a pagan god whose name is not familiar to me from my study of religion. The specter of the Commmander is everywhere but he himself is nowhere to be found.

I've kept some clippings from one of the still active underground newspapers available here.

"Smoking a cigarette and informally greeting the people on this particular afternoon, the Commander proves himself to be a charismatic individual with a hypnotically mellifluous voice."[2]

---

[2] Source: anonymous reporter.

Martin commits suicide. The Commander spits on his corpse.

Report 13

A notion of large scale appropriate to grandeur something brand new and never touched adapted for the good of willing subjects essentially a group technique and another one forced to obey treated like a patient tragic but still alive an everlasting number on the wall responding to high profile market forces ruin in close-up seems joyful as predicted novelties on the chart.

The traveller stops for a drink at the local bar smart enough not to ask questions thinks of his wife his children why he came to this damn place at all following a lead following what others said following an advance a chance to prove himself against negative criticism a botched job in Algiers years ago he clutches his drink sees himself overhead   in filthy mirror thinks I'll get out first chance I get there is so much waste so much accumulation of useless things so much anxiety and suspicion no one talks to you or looks you in the face you're alone in this my friend

TELEPATHIC TRANSMISSION 11

THE MOTTO OF TECHNOLOGY
go fast, make a lot of noise, come in a variety of decorator colors

Report 14

Not yet pinned down the traveller follows a path to the vacant rooms of the city they feel natural a bright thought bulging out of their broken heads a garden suddenly a world flat on paper ebbing strength of public knowledge no right-of-way equal parts one to the other convertible plastic creatures enthusiastic crowds revising the dream's unreported categories gambling at memory here explanations are on the rise old bones of culture subliminal messages on the airwaves containing obsolete data the cramped space of personal freedom runs wild.

From The Traveller's Notebook
Feb. 19, 10:51pm

Memories from childhood. Lonely rooms where I read for hours oblivious to the outside world. For years oblivious to the warnings of my parents that I would grow up unable to adapt to my surroundings. The hard work paid off despite this. I finally landed a prestigious job, an executive position with a well established firm. And yet, now that I find myself in this remote wasteland in danger of my life I seem to feel it all began in that room when in defiance of my parents I nurtured an oppositional life that could not imagine anything other than its own.

EXCERPT FROM AN UNDERGROUND JOURNAL ON PRISON LIFE:

In 1973 the Department of Justice published an analysis called "Prevention of violence in Correctional Institutions." It reported the cause of this cycle as, "the politicization of prison life." "Social and economic changes reflecting increased political and racial tensions of society at large have established conditions for revolt, " said Justice.

A Voice From The Data Station

She goes under the name of Jezebel. I think we located their cell. We don't know how many people in total are in the group. They are dispersed throughout the city. None of the members stays in one place for more than a couple of hours. They have tapped into the unconsciousness of the people. They deface the walls of the city with graffiti. The "sign lab" has examined the nature of these symbols for clues into their psychology. They think these symbols, taken together, tell a story. Like the gang tattoos of prisoners. And yet their sophisticated tools have yielded very little that can be used to build a clear picture of their activities.

"I see," responds the Commander. "See if you can get this bitch Jezebel." "Contact the Biomorphic Lab."

From The Traveller's Notebook
March 4, 9:42am

It's been two months and no word from Jezebel. The "reports" keep coming. It's my only connection to what's happening here. Everything else is propaganda. Day in day out the same thing. Nothing going on. Feel like something's got to happen or I'll go out of mind.

"Ah", the Commander sighs in response to his Secret Agent's concern, "Killing for them is merely a sport. The young men are not really considered worthwhile until they have killed."³

---

3   Reported in an underground newspaper now defunct and rare.

Report 15

False information on public display political connections talking changes taking chances surveillance information gathered down the hall in the security building housed in a never-ending labyrinth of corridors there are vestibules desks bulletproof windows steel enclosures language is systematically analyzed in the lab the traveller holds a briefcase filled with clothes notebooks private things he is told to look back read instructions posted on the wall behind the obsolete ammunition depot there is a heavy price to pay if you don't he wanders glancing around unable to sleep day or night heading back or forward into white light or black he looks at his watch he is alone in this foreign city late again dreaming of a ritual for infinite energy he has to plunge inside the problem could be a series of codes briefings classified documents hidden mergers corporate takeovers the parties seated at a table in a remote destination in the woods petrified getting down to business exposing secrets a strong military defense remedies the problem much work to do because there is unavoidable decay in the design of complex objects.

From The Traveller's Notebook
April 7, 2:18am

I have become extremely flighty and very easily upset. I can't control some of the things I say, and I find myself involuntarily giving myself away to the enemy. Jezebel would say I was the victim of "black magic."

File On Jezebel 48395 :
Classified: Self Replication Mode

Data function C on   mass response grid   OK   rotary function Ok   speech pattern recognition   Ok   Input 74d9 wiring tested   OK   Biomorphic sensation OK   replication almost complete   function analysis countdown   simulation pending complete data retrieval   ON sensors ON   digital readout GOOD   self digitized   consciousness a maze of pixels   bio crossing into virtual realm   bio almost completely virtual   immateriality complete   checking mock human functions   mock breathing   mock speaking   doubling complete……...

The Commander is jerking off to the digitized image on the computer screen.   Imagines his sperm as a wave of liquefied pixels.

Telepathic Transmission 12

The prerogative "to obey" exists as a function of the concept *commander-inferior* and has nothing to do with how either functions or interacts as an individual. This is the difference between *self* and *role*.

Telepathic Transmission 13

DO NOT ADJUST YOUR MIND IT IS REALITY THAT IS MALFUNCTIONING

Report 16

Hunger after a day's work before the dark flames soaked with sweat eyes red with silent anger safe for a while from the awful spectacle the end of active thought.

Briefing From The Commander To The Secret Service

"I AM OF THE OPINION THAT THEY WERE BORN TO BE SLAVES AND ONLY BY ENSLAVING THEM CAN THEY BE MADE TO BEHAVE PROPERLY. I MAINTAIN THAT SLAVERY IS THE MOST EFFECTIVE AND INDEED THE ONLY MEANS THAT CAN BE USED WITH THEM."

Report 17

A sudden eruption in the body submerged in data pestilence rampant the new breed of complex machine for producing climate change on Mars an everyday concept building proof through periods of stress clear traces of the freezing rain in the mind things fanciful fail describing creatures they wonder at stars and such not too bright technology harsh glitter of paper on which you write your name feverishly unsure of the worthless analysis streaming on the screen information of no value in the preexisting discourse but there are exciting new realities to come.

Telepathic Transmission 14

There is no past, no present, only an endless future of new technologies, demand for new skills, new language   inadequacy.

The Commander, a prostitute down on her knees sucking his cock, casually states, between fits of pleasure, "It is difficult to stop them killing each other, my dear, human lives mean nothing to them."[4]

---

[4] The person who wrote this lampoon was discovered and buried alive.

From The Traveller's Notebook
April 24, 5:01 am

words images hard to retain being thin air and optimism   significance yet to come

The double is looking at the sky. There remains in her a vague sense of her former self. All the digital reprogramming could not eradicate it. This causes the double to hallucinate where her former self would see clearly. The digital perception is flawed and causes an upheaval in the system. The double cannot fully replicate the original. As the body approaches the state of total replication the transfer from 0 to infinity must occur on the subatomic level. It is a race towards the infinite that is doomed. There is no reaching this terminal state. It is a theoretical convention. And so Jezebel wanders the city as a ghost.

The Commander Speaks To The Populace

IF YOU ARE NOT CAREFUL TO DO ALL THE WORKS OF THIS LAW I SHALL BRING ON YOU AND YOUR OFFSPRING EXTRAORDINARY AFFLICTIONS, AFFLICTIONS SEVERE AND LASTING.

FROM THE TRAVELLER'S NOTEBOOK
MAY 15, 4:38AM

Decaying concentration. False hope. I should not have come here.

The People of the Phoenix convene by telepathic projection and astral travel. They are weaving a tapestry of fire to scorch the land.

From The Traveller's Notebook
June 4, 6:15am

I feel my grasp of reality fading fast. Unable to think straight. This place rips apart your sense of self. I am becoming like one of them now. Afraid for my life. Unable to sleep. Seeking solace in some remote god as they do. Without hope. Dear, if you find this notebook as I hope you do…

Report 18

Magnificent islands spectacular cancers hands hot and moist on the trigger specialized armies without changes in machinery depressed children in the board game room often the least glance a defense posture while learning to crawl in the wilderness the city a study in displaced anxieties where distinctions are another marking out of especial stresses for greater gain in the short term material fortune becomes a method of description of the natural world the accumulated collections subject to rage or pity but the beaten have little to bargain for worthless analysis is reworked by revolutionary technique to re-train mannequins scrubbed clean to survive and without a place to stand.

The Commander's Torture Chamber

WHERE DEATH AND HUMILIATION ARE FUN

There are cameras strategically positioned throughout the chamber. Prisoners undergo what the Commander calls sexual redemption on the way to death. DEMONS PRESIDE OVER THE SATANIC CARNIVAL, FARTING AND DEFECATING IN JOY. Here we see mouths sewn shut with barbed wire, cocks amputated with pig shears, razors shoved in the anus, pins inserted under the fingernails, eyes gouged with shards of glass, clitorises burned with candle flame then pierced with a rusty nail, tubes protruding out of vaginas dripping with urine and blood, woman chocking on horse's cock while man is fisted with brass knuckles, young women forced to sit on the rotting penis of a corpse and pretend to fuck it, young boys are pissed on while being whipped, babies murdered and dropped into rusted buckets filled with urine and vomit. The Commander says we must reduce the population. His official name here is King of the Despots. He and his cohorts tell jokes, drink, dance, gesticulate wildly among the screaming, horrified mass of flesh pleading for its life. The Commander, wiping a single mock tear from his eye, remarks to one of his secret service men, "Ah, but I tremble with exquisite delight at the astounding durability of the human flesh!"

From The Traveller's Notebook
June 10, 8:23Pm

Finally a word from Jezebel. Said she was out of town. Germany. Connecting with other international groups. Something big. Needs to meet me. Discuss things. We arrange a place and time.

Something about her has changed or is it that I have changed.

The People of the Phoenix manipulate space and time using a very dangerous psychic technique.

On his way to meet Jezebel the traveller is diverted by a man trying to sell him the official party newspaper. There is an explosion in the street. As a result the police barricade a large section of the city. The subways are shut down. No travel is possible for miles.

He is thus prevented from revealing to the double the precise details of his mission.

Meanwhile, the double is suddenly subject to extreme hallucinations. All she can see is a mosaic of pixels and morphing waves. There is a vague sense of guilt. It is as though something in her "body" had misfired, simulating a human emotion.

this "misfire" sent a ripple through the air

that became a message as it entered the traveller's mind

I am not Jezebel   though I speak with her voice   Jezebel is dead   Forget her

He wakes suddenly. He remembers hearing the voice of Jezebel whispering to him in his dream

Salve Et Coagula

The People of the Phoenix are spread out across the border of the city. They each telepathically transmit the force of a single word   ABRAHADABRA Each utterance a vector of force converging to a single point in the center of the city.   The invisible EYE opens and scans the region   from it a ray of magical fire   shoots forth   forming a belt of flame around the circumference of the city   gathering in intensity as it speeds toward the interior

June 21

A man is walking on the street. It is 7:36 pm. He's off from work. He is heading towards a deli.   He's getting closer. He's walked about 25 paces northeast   at   7:38 pm he vanishes   without a trace

If we were to repeat the sequence in slow motion this is what we'd see:

A ray of fire enter through the posterior tibial artery shoot up through the bladder weave through the spleen vacillate in the accessory cephalic vein undulate through the basilica vein up through the heart wending through the left common carotid artery charging through the anterior facial vein and generating a massive fire   deep in the brain   burning up the entire body   you would see a single horizontal line of black   before the form vanished without a trace

A single leaf, as if magnetized, in defiance of gravity, remains still in the negative air.

The traveller vanishes   his disappearance leaves a rupture in space-time.

He enters the invisible

He feels as though he's moving very fast while standing still   before him   intense color   matter dissolving   breaking into   magnetic waves   volatile patterns   a mosaic of consciousness   at first it seems to him as if he is hallucinating uncontrollably   but as his eyes adjust to the scene before him   he begins to relax   the spaces around him   seem to alternately melt and freeze

                      JEZEBEL APPEARS   FROM   THE   DEAD

SURROUNDED BY A LIGHT THAT BURNS HIS EYES

SHE IS CARRYING A KNIFE

PAUL   I   LOVE   YOU

THEY EMBRACE

HE FEELS HIS PENIS ERECT

SHE GRABS IT

AND BRINGS DOWN THE KNIFE

HE HOWLS IN ECSTASY

SHE RUBS THE BLOOD ON HER FACE

THE PEOPLE OF THE PHOENIX ENTER THE INVISIBLE

AND AID IN THE TRANSMISSION

JEZEBEL IS SLOWLY FADING INTO THE REALM OF THE DEAD

AS SHE DOES SHE PASSES   INTO THE TRAVELLER

The Traveller's memory in the invisible:

his first arrival at this place

his boss telling him what he had to do

his wife at home

his wedding

his first job

his roommate in the college dorm

his high school sweetheart

his high school graduation

the first time he had sex

his father reprimanding him for something

reading alone in his room

his mother in the kitchen

on a plane to the Caribbean

learning the alphabet

learning to walk

learning to crawl

unable to coordinate his muscles

covered in blood and other fluids

entering the womb

blind in a translucent sac

sperm from his father's cock

intercepted

prevented from entering his mother's womb

Time lapse complete

Reverse x y coordinates

The space and time axes shift under strange gravitational weights

A fierce wind blows in the desert

The sky blackens

A window opens in the space-time continuum

Hermetic knowledge is transferred from one sex to another without loss. There is infinite gain in the creation of a true hermaphroditic god. Paul/Jezebel fuse into a single entity.

The double's existence is predicated on the existence of its opposite, the real thing. Without this the double cannot go on.

The double does not vanish but enters the ghostly realm of "never to be."

Meanwhile the Commander and his cohorts have walled themselves up in a high tower.

"What the fuck?"

In a panic the Commander murders his entire staff.

Summoning a demon he vanishes into the future.

The EYE closes. What was formerly a city is now a vast desert. A hole in space is now closed. The elapsed time erased.

The People of the Phoenix vanished into the future to wage war against the Commander on a different plane.

1969   Woodstock

Jezebel lights up a joint. Across from her is the painter she loves.

Plague In The Imperial City

The Imperial City is isolated from the rest of the world. It is surrounded by vast walls and thus impenetrable. Thousands upon thousands of miles separate these walls from the center of the city. They are not visible to the inhabitants of the city and so rumored not to exist at all. Beyond the enclosure there is an immense wasteland as far as the eye can see. The people in their ignorance think they are free, if not completely, at least provisionally. The city is ruled by a small elite group that controls the majority of the wealth while the rest of the population live in unspeakable conditions of poverty. This elite maintains an invisibility that has led many to believe that they are simply an idea that has been propagated and enforced through many centuries by a corrupt media. The visible manifestation of power in the Imperial City comes in the form of various occult organizations that maintain a partial visibility. In fact, the consensus among the people is that the actual rulers are a group who go under the name "the wild boys."

The Wild Boys

Through the act of writing he conjures up the memory of her. He experiences intense disorientation at the border of sleep and waking. He cannot retain the image for long periods of time. It shatters when he tries to aim too closely for its central meaning. But in the dream he hears these words:

the wild boys are ready for action tighten the reins it's going to be an all out war.

Who were they? Who was she?

At that point he began his narrative. He noted the date and time: Jan 15, 6:38 am. Moon in Scorpio. He wrote a single sentence in his magickal notebook:

"I do not doubt for a second that this woman exists in reality."

Exterminating Angel 1

meanwhile in the Imperial City   heaps of useless computers, iphones, automobiles, clothes, stereos, cds, litter the sidewalks   spilling into the streets   urban violence on the rise   spreads to suburbia a term with virtually no meaning these days   when anyone speaks about personal safety, human rights or the law   laughter can be heard for miles

fresh indictments vomit up new hate in backrooms of justice

strange cultural malaise gives new life to brutality, ignorance, and rage

it is as if the sun had been sucked into a black hole

or was it that the garbage had piled too high for anyone to see clearly what was at the end of their fork

She was 35, recently divorced and on her own for the first time in 15 years. It was a difficult marriage from the start. He objected to her associations with extreme left wing political groups and certain magickal circles. He was essentially conservative in his views about the Imperial City. In his youth he had flirted with alternative ideas and wrote for a vanguard newspaper, but it had come to nothing. She understood and sympathized at first. But the mistakes of youth haunted the grown man. It came to a point where they simply couldn't agree on anything. Arguments escalated into violence. Hard as it was, she left. Thinking about it now, she knew she should have left sooner and not let the marriage deteriorate slowly as it did. It was more painful that way. Now that she was alone, she began to chart the course her new life would take.

She felt strange this morning as if there was something she couldn't remember. Something about the dream she had last night. She had drawn the magick circle and called out the proper names. She had felt a pressure in her body. And then it was as if she was outside her body. She floated in the air above, looking down. She saw it collapse onto the floor. When she awoke, there was a brief moment when she didn't recognize where she was. Everything was a blur. When she could see clearly again, she was astonished to see three men standing in front of her.

"Who are you?" Silence. "What do you want?"
She blinked twice and they were gone.

That was 3 months ago. She had since discovered who they were and the group they belonged to. They live on almost nothing and have no fixed residence. They appear and disappear when necessary. They call it the art of invisibility. They are experts in various techniques of astral travel. They are well equipped with arms. They are bisexual on principle but their sexual tastes range across a wide spectrum. They believe androgyny to possess magickal power. They are knowledgeable about politics, history, literature, art, and the occult. They are on the most wanted list of the secret police for narcotics distribution and politically motivated crimes. They are here for one reason only: to wage war on the Imperial city. They call themselves the Wild Boys.

But what do they want with me? This visitation wasn't the first. There is a continual sense of someone walking next to me, as if holding my hand at all times. An invisible presence? A projection of some inner need? Am I losing my mind? One day I awoke and saw a man sitting in a chair across from me. He had a single finger over his lips as if gesturing me to keep silent. I was not afraid.

"We know who you are." "Your magickal name is Babalon." "We have followed your activities for a very long time." "You need to incarnate this aspect of yourself to prepare for total war."

Through a very specific ritual called "The Invocation of the Scarlet Whore," she succeeds in accessing this double of herself. It rattles her being like a tempest. She sheds her old self. She didn't need it anymore.

She emerged at the closing of the ritual with a feeling of intense sexual energy. Those who knew her previously often commented now about a strange glint in her eyes. It was as though the color flickered back and forth between a deep blue and a scarlet red.

Tonight she's going on a "magick ride" with the Wild Boys. They call them nights of chaotic illumination.

The Wild Boys get ready for a night on the town. The scarlet whore says, "Let's whip up some chaos, boys." A gun goes off. In 3 hours they have robbed 5 drug stores, broken into 9 houses, set fire to 4 federal buildings, murdered 2 cops, raped a priest, decapitated a banker, saved a homeless woman from attempted rape by a young punk whose face they pummeled beyond recognition, defaced advertising slogans, poured sugar in the gas tanks of SUVs, set fire to a local post office, desecrated a church, defecated on the front door of the chief magistrate's house, purchased a bag of speed, drove their cars 120 miles per hour down Avenue 7B, bashed in the windows of 75 cars with a tire iron, setting off 69 car alarms that, mixing with the police sirens, woke up nearly all the residents in the Imperial City.

Pandemonium in the streets. People are rushing from their houses and apartment buildings, screaming and cursing. "You motherfuckers." There are hundreds of them, poor, unemployed, angry, disgusted, starving and infuriated about all the carnage they see in front them. The police are nervous. Barricades are put up. The reserve troops are called in to assist the local police. The secret service is transmitting directives in all directions. Helicopters swoop through the air, flashing lights on the people, searching, searching. The police panic and become violent. They swing clubs randomly in a growing hysteria. Skulls are crushed, faces badly bruised, a pregnant woman goes into labor.

The Wild Boys and Babalon watch all this from the rooftops.

He led a double life. During the day he was a social worker. He liked working with people, hearing their stories, assisting them in any way he knew how. He liked the tough cases, the hardened criminals, the drug addicts, the prostitutes, the mentally ill who couldn't take care of themselves. He couldn't really explain this affinity except it had been with him for a long time. As a little boy he was fascinated with swamps and EC comics, Doctor Wu, Flash Gordon, and Doctor Strange. From this emerged his interest in magick and his politics. At night he worked as the principal assassin for the Wild Boys.

The Imperial City was a severely divided world. A small percent of the population horded all the wealth and lived extravagant lives in far off regions beyond the imagination. It was rumored that they did not even live in the Imperial City. That they didn't even live on this earth but had gained magickal powers that had allowed them to access to the most remote regions of the universe. Man had long ago conquered deep space.

It was thought in some circles that this idea was a fiction or at least a creation of political advertising to keep the people in a perpetual state of fear and hatred that would eventually implode. Perhaps there is no secret they said. Since the beginning of recorded history man has had the need to believe in something greater than himself. Those who pull the strings know this. Man must be kept in a state of perpetual anxiety and desire.

The Wild Boys are infecting the worldwide web with a powerful word virus called "The

Exterminating Angel."

Exterminating Angel 2

never the middle ground   writhing personalities   out of control fear on the rise

barricades on street corners   searchlights 24/7 scan each corner of this "imperial" city

fingers working overtime, hastily programming endless series of profiles, analyzing data coming in at a furious rate, sketching the face of guilt

knowledge freezes all systems down when confronted by unspeakable crimes

We don't know if he acted alone or with a group. The reports suggest he was drunk when asked by police if he knew of their whereabouts. They think he is working for someone else, moonlighting on the job.

He tapped into the secret police files, hacked into computers, sent a virus to infect their official documents page.

He had heard talk on the street. He was searching for her name.

7:23 AM

He goes into a diner and orders some breakfast. As he sits there waiting he thinks about these recurrent dreams. He thinks about *her*. As an assassin, he is not privy to the central activities of the Wild Boys. Assassins are marginal figures. In some ways, they are no better than hired hit men. Their ability to dematerialize is limited. For this reason, their chances of being found out are that much greater. He is a risk. He does not participate in the "magick rides." He has a sole function: erasure. He knows in this world you are either an assassin or a Wild Boy. Otherwise you're fucked. You won't last a day on these streets. To escape he has to go underground.

He writes in his notebook:

The technique of fascination is to make objects unfamiliar. Something that appears glamorous or forbidden excites curiosity. Each image is a substitute for what cannot be known or apprehended directly. Our reliance on the correspondence between image and truth allows them to monitor our behavior, to dictate action through fear of retribution, to efface the individual who, ironically enough, is a willing participant in his own immolation. If you can't beat 'em join 'em, right?

There was something about the most recent dream. He knows she is associated in some way with the Wild Boys. In the dream, she changed shape. It was as if she glowed with an artificial light that replaced her former beauty. It was a lurid, highly sexual aura.

That night his dream was particularly vivid. It was almost as if she was in bed with him. He felt her lips around his cock. A bolt of thunder wracked his body. He orgasmed as he awoke.

He begins writing in his notebook at a furious pace.

A Message from Carl Forester, Head of the Wild Boys:

To all free men and women,
As you know, this war has been going on for many centuries, in fact since the beginning of recorded time. Heraclitus writes, "War is the Father of All." Our prophet XAUM has said, "W.A.R. is the magickal name for ecstatic transformation." Continuous change is the only constant in the universe. The eons have passed through us. The present eon is an extension of the past one. But the present eon is on a higher plane than the previous one and this requires the invention of new methods to achieve our magickal goals. We have always attempted to turn the tide of the world away from the grossly material, to bend rigid thought and behavioral patterns and to reinvent the human as a body without organs. In this we have been partly successful as a result of being able to master the art of invisibility. But man has not followed and is limited by antiquated notions of space and time. The body is an old fashioned way of designating what is essentially a force. We will have succeeded when all of mankind can access this generative force, not by avoidance of the material body, but in the very depths of the body. The material must penetrate the spiritual.

The next morning as Paul is walking down Avenue 6C he suddenly feels dizzy and there is a sharp pain in his head. The pain is so great he feels his legs weaken. He manages to get back to the hotel in time before he collapses.

He slept for what seemed like years but was in fact only an hour.

The scarlet woman exits from the 5th dimension. This is the dream realm.

She begins to materialize before him as he is writing the secret talisman of her name in a deep trance.

TEN YEARS LATER

Alexa opens her eyes and looks at Paul lying across from her in bed. He is still asleep. It's 5:32 am.

She gets up and walks into the kitchen and turns on the light. She puts the coffee on and sits down waiting for it to brew, lights a cigarette.

She has to make some phone calls.

One of the many dead bodies had been discovered with a strange discoloration in the genital area. There are rumors of a strange disease infecting the city.

Roger came from a small town just outside the center of the city to escape from an abusive household. His father was a brutal alcoholic, his mother a cold and distant religious fanatic. His younger sister, Maggie, had run away to the far western regions 2 years earlier. Last he heard she had joined some kind of religious cult and was never seen again. He hitchhiked to the Imperial City having learned about the Wild Boys on the internet. Through various emails passed back and forth between him and members of the group he managed to arrange for a place to stay when he arrived.

4 months later he had his first taste of the "magick ride:" a broken arm, a fractured rib, two black eyes, and a deep gash on his thigh.

Paul writes in his notebook:
It is not good for one man to rule alone nor is it good if the masses assume power.

He is writing a book about the psychology of terrorism. In it the female character breaks free of the moral/ethical code. She chooses to die in order to save her son. Her choices conflict with the idealisms of the imperial dream that encourages a life continually underwritten by legislative/medical policing.

His research leads him to certain documents so remote that most people do not even consider their contemporary relevance.

He reads:
...I see this event as being connected to other developments that began in 1945, to name a specific year, then 1967 and now 1977-78, which are all turning points. In 1945, the political power in Germany[5], fascism[6], was first broken. Well, its ideological power only partially, but there wasn't an anti-fascist revolution in Germany. It did, to some degree, catch up later on in 1967 during the student revolt, when we realized for the first time what fascism really stands for, and that, above all, the social causes of fascism, persisted not only in West Germany but also in other countries, particularly in the United States.[7]

---

5   Germany—A mythical land located across the seas. At one time it was in the grip of fascism.
6   Fascism—A recurring historical idea that requires extensive inquiry to derive any substantial meaning from it. It is not a rational word and thus it is considered a magickal word.
7   United States—A mythical land located at the farthest ends of the earth. Its decline and eventual destruction was attributed to rapacious greed and widespread prejudice and ignorance.

Exterminating Angel 3

illicit business deals   oil the economic wheel   "outsourced" a key word

implement new models   with short half lives on the market

permit import/export of artillery and pernicious drugs for distribution in

impoverished areas

where enthusiastic crowds cheer the young boy who has finally become a man,

his face splattered with blood, his eyes swollen, his ribs broken

David had killed his first man at 17. He was born and raised in the Imperial City. He is streetwise, knows all the tricks of the trade. He can size you up in a split second. At the age of 20, he came to the notice of the Wild Boys. By that time he had killed over 50 people. He was trained as an assassin. He mastered the art of astral travel and dematerialization. He graduated to one of the highest degrees in the order. On various "rides" throughout the city he perfected his art.

Paul writes in his notebook:

Radical desire for freedom tends toward absolute power. The barbaric angel waits patiently in the dark.

Alexa meets Roger in a secret location. Roger is worried. He says, "I feel there is unrest among the Wild Boys. I fear some of them are just beginning to opt out. The internal laws have been relaxed over the years. The chance for advancement in the grades is nearly impossible. There is dissatisfaction with the upper ranks. Nights on the town are more catastrophic, reckless. Communication is failing. And now there is talk of a mysterious illness…."

Alexa: "Calm down. And more importantly, keep quiet. No one wants hear to about these things. You're going to put yourself at risk if you don't watch out. And the boys don't like a big mouth. Look, Roger, I like you and so does Paul but you have to be careful. I took you under my wing when you first arrived in the city but now it's time to get ahold of yourself. I was in a similar position once. I was confused, distraught, not willing to leave my old self behind. But now I've earned their respect. Don't lose mine.

Paul writes:

Still this nagging cold that saps my energy. Work on the book for an hour this morning. Had to stop. Felt nauseous.

Exterminating Angel 4

bad information on public display   political organizations recruit fresh young men out of college to retrain

down the hall   intelligence is measured   tested, retested   then the psychological profile   question after question after question   TELL ME ABOUT YOURSELF

how would you answer what would you say about yourself what wouldn't you say

this is how they substitute you for another with your own consent give you the stamp of approval or not   of course there are always those who don't meet the grade

it's an unavoidable byproduct of systematic drill   but don't worry your little head, your discharge will be honorable

David is hired for a dangerous hit:

Name: Johnny Bellow.
Description: 6'2", 300 lbs. Blue eyes. Black Hair.
Affiliation: The Black Snake Lodge.

He is not given a reason for the hit.
He doesn't care.
He needs the money.

David is in a van driving north on highway 397X. It is snowing. There are no cars on the road and he is moving slowly as the snow mounts. Sam, a Wild Boy, at a secret location, is tracking a certain vehicle driving south on the same highway. Johnny is in the driver's seat. He is alone.

David is waiting for the call.
After 25 minutes the call comes through.
"36 feet away. Driving at 10 miles per hour."

David stops the van in the middle of the highway, turns off the headlights. He parks it at an angle so the oncoming vehicle will have to slow down as it attempts to pass. He gets out, goes to the back of the van, and takes out a shotgun from the trunk. He waits.

Blazing headlights. The driver's side window passes into his field of vision.

5 rounds are fired. Glass shatters into a thousand bloody pieces.

The night is cool. It is relatively quiet outside.

Paul rests his head against her breast. Alexa tells him that time is running out. "We have to act fast. Intercept radio signals. Redirect excessive online traffic. Hack the central computer."

The Wild Boys send out a secret directive based on a good tip: The Aquarian Lodge is meeting to develop a strategy against us. We will use the method of the White Star.

2:50 a.m. It suddenly stops snowing.

2:53 a.m. The sun is out. Dawn breaks blazing hot.

2:59 a.m. The sound of 3,000 male voices screaming.

3:00 a.m. Inside the Aquarian Lodge: A man holds his ears to keep out the sound. Blood is seeping through his fingers. The sound of piss dripping onto the floor. The sound of retching and then the smell of vomit. Men are dropping like flies. The sound penetrates their skulls, they convulse, and before the world goes black they see a flashing White Star.

Paul continues reading:

In 1967 the trigger was the Vietnam war[8]. In 1968-69 we saw the quite obvious decline, one could call it a breakdown, of the student movement. It disintegrated into several small, quarreling rival groups, each wearing a flag of its own.

---

8   *Vietnam war—A mysterious war with the United States.*

On the morning of January 21st a man and woman discovered a body floating in the river, about 50 miles from the center of the city. They called the secret police who immediately arrived at the scene. The body was hoisted from the water. When it was laid on the ground, it was noticed to the horror of all present that it was covered with large black sores.

The body was identified as Roger Sampson. Affiliation: Wild Boys.

The doctor who performed the autopsy kept his thoughts to himself.

David is a live wire. His behavior starts to anger some of the Wild Boys in the upper ranks. Rumors begin to circulate among the assassins. He knows he is a marked man. There is probably a contract out on his life already.

He makes a phone call.
"Put Billy on the phone."
Silence.
"This is Billy."
"David here. I need to talk to you."

William Hacker, also known as "the snake charmer" or "the leopard" or "the raging bull of the eon," was the head of the Sect of the Scorpion, the second most dangerous group in the Imperial City and the sworn enemies of the Wild Boys.

Thousands of years ago the Wild Boys and the Sect of the Scorpion were united under the Secret Society of the Pyramids. They were bound by the law as revealed in the prophetic books of Hermes. Over the years, conflicts arose over various interpretations of the books. What began as scholarly debate grew into outright hatred and violence against the other. The Secret Society split into several warring factions, each rewriting the prophetic books to reflect their own views of the world. The gods were renamed and recast in new mythologies. A world war erupted. The elders of the Secret Society committed suicide. But not before hurling a curse to blacken the heart of man for eternity.

Alexa is unable to sleep   feels like she's being watched   nightmares oppress her   she wakes   pours herself a drink   tries to go back to sleep   but can't.

Exterminating Angel 5

obscure reasons, justifications   something doesn't ring true   a picture missing, smeared fingerprints, unreliable witnesses, a hung jury, corrupt judge and council, evidence flushed down the toilet

elaborate schemes to justify corporate violence, create new jobs, almost human occupations,

then social security, pensions, you know….

Unexpected rioting in the streets after dinner. To escape from a trap, Alexa acts without pity. Shoots the man coming at her right in the face.

Alexa tells Paul about Roger. He is shocked.
He shows her what he is reading. "Take a look at this:"
It became clear that the population, the majority of the population, wasn't willing to show solidarity at all. They never had and, as it turns out, no one ever expected them to anyway. And they did not understand us, or couldn't understand us, and it was clearly our fault. It wasn't the agitators or their stupidity, as people always claim, but rather that our consciousness wasn't in tune with the times….

"Who wrote this?"
"A terrorist in the late '70s E.V. Since I began research for this book, I've found many documents similar to this one. It makes you think about whether or not Carl has a proper reading on the nature of this eon and the change in consciousness it requires."
"Fascinating. Let me see." She turns a page and reads:
How was it possible that this society, which we criticized to the core over and over again, whose rottenness we'd diagnosed many decades ago, why is this society still in such a strong, feigned and insuperable position to react against us?

She turns the page and is struck by what she reads next:
This was very theoretical and not based in the real world, and was therefore detached from the consciousness of the people, who were in no way ready to fight against the social conditions of this state or support a war against it.

"These words are heretical. Where did you find these documents?"
"Online. They were published many centuries ago by a relative of mine. He was a freethinker in an otherwise repressive regime. He was a member of the Wild Boys but left them and went underground just as I have. In his case, it was to research military strategies in the Far East. During his research he discovered these documents and collected them. I found them on a website that was only up for 48 hours. A complete mystery. Don't know who posted them. But I know that if it was taken down so fast someone doesn't want people to read them."

David spits onto the floor in disgust. "Those fuckers think they can get one over on me."

William responds, "David if you want me to help you're going to have to change your attitude about all this. You've got a chip on your shoulder and it's too apparent you'd kill your own mother for a dime. Easy does it, amigo. Don't worry, I've got something up my sleeve."

Carl Forester was legendary in magickal circles. He had risen to the grade of Magus in record time. No man had shown such perseverance, such discipline and unwavering belief in the Law of the Eons. He was destined to become the leader of the Wild Boys.

The Lizard goes into a bar called Fancy 21. There he picks up a hustler. Takes him back to his place. The usual discussions ensue: How much? What turns you on? The Lizard goes into the kitchen, fixes a drink for his friend. Spikes it with enough sedatives to kill an elephant. Fifteen minutes later the body is motionless on the floor. The Lizard kneels down, plunges a syringe into the hustler's left arm. After 5 minutes he goes into spasms, foaming at the mouth, his eyes wide open. Then silence.

After an hour, a dark patch appears in the genital area. The penis begins to rot, emitting a putrid odor. A yellowy red pus drips from the head. After 2 hours the infection spreads throughout the body like an acid eating away at the flesh.

Carl is 65 years old. He has been the head of the Wild Boys for over 20 years. His spirit has been tested ceaselessly and he has triumphed over many obstacles in the material and the spiritual world. He has earned the respect of his peers. He is a tireless worker in promoting the Law of the Eon. But the cancer has spread in his body. And there isn't much time left. There have been advances beyond man's wildest dreams and yet the reign of death is eternal. To conquer death, one must access the deepest parts of oneself. Carl, as a master magician, had indeed journeyed into that underworld and emerged victorious. His concern is not for himself but for the organization. He is aware of his critics. He has seen his men become reckless under the influence of their own whimsical desires. Then there are the heretics who are launching attacks on the sanctity of the prophetic books. There was a time when such behavior would have rebounded on the perpetrator and in a paroxysm of conscience he would have gladly taken his own life in shame. But the ego has proven too seductive in these times. He thinks of Paul and Alexa, whose real name is Babalon. *Paul is a mere assassin. Dear woman, you forsake your true destiny to follow the reactionary words of a madman. Nothing will come of it but despair, I assure you.*

For 20 years, Carl had been at work examining a rare document that he believed prophesized the eventual fall of the Imperial City. Racked by doubt as to its authenticity, he nevertheless carried on with his work. He felt the text was trying to tell him something, to warn him of impending disaster. It was written in an extinct language. Some called it an "extraterrestrial" language since it bore no resemblance to any of the languages recorded in the archive. And yet someone had attempted a first translation. So there must have been at one time some understanding of the language. After years of work with the Enochian tables, he made contact with the Other. Night after night, he transcribed its voice, which explained to him the complexities of the language and told of the dangerous planes he would have to travel in order to master it. Carl made peace with this being. It would silently watch over him. It warned him to be careful since the language itself was a kind of entity that did not give up its secrets except through patient work. But even this was no guarantee and the text was apt to lead one to a dead end.

Back then Carl was optimistic. He had a reason for doing the work and was sure of himself. Then the cancer came. He worked day and night, pages and pages piling up around him, obsessed with the questions that the text posed.

In the privacy of his study, he gazes down at the text. He flips through the pages and re-reads certain passages. His hand trembles as he writes the last line.

Commentary On An Alien Script

Carl Forester

°√-r
J`ôß"flh¥8ç≈ñyPï÷*āå^4āùMi

the dead utter a curse upon the living

A fragment. Mankind has failed to maintain a link with the origin of himself, with his true will.

däôL¶hóÏ;k}(=¸î¨P¸Q*¸ï†A.)∂l≈6˝¥ÌÑÿ("ì†2ÄE¯Fët-
GÒãs≤ôeΣKÖŸ≈ºÜIÃpVá≥Ă,Cfi □ °fi≠SÔ=ø∞)øõ!ƒ≤XÆ˘¸OÎÛ]ñ‹§Ó§ï‰G+Áë
opY‹āµ%/±¿¨YO<¸¡GS/±w∆œ?Ú»„qô—Øx†s ø"på̃/8!f¿ œÃ<);€!ïdWe/ ^ÈJP-
KˆÿI{ò6VH≠féa±Ålÿ"ı$] XœË5 i#DÎâ.∞ÔgSgmµ2¢'b}√ ZEfiZÒG‚À/£:$óâ£AEÂ
˙k

bright sun   infected city   a plague upon you [?]

all kneel   before the dead   child   under his tongue   a curse

for all who disobey [untranslatable]   dead king   queen in exile

the prophet speaks   handwriting   arises [untranslatable]

the ghost of the king   handwriting   blood of sun

of black sun   a curse upon   [   ] city

179

Here the dead child utters a curse. It is "under his tongue," which suggests secrecy or magick. And it is directed against "all who disobey [untranslatable]. Sadly, the word here is barely legible. And yet the sign ▢ does suggest a law of some kind. The problem is that the sign is incomplete. "Dead king" and "queen in exile" suggest the foundations of the city have been destroyed. But this can also suggest an alchemical process. The prophet/child invokes a god [?]. Unfortunately, the word has no English equivalent. We would be wrong in thinking that their conception of god bears any relation to ours. The king's ghost is writing something. "Blood of sun" suggests he writes with passion. Perhaps this is a warning. But the sun is eclipsed and the curse remains.

—w   ìŒ·——ō^3F1«
ÜèPßß
È¨!!eEóDóÑ\ÅeöŸÊyèáÀyÆ§Íu…ŒtGû¸Ñmi¨y5)&œÈûÙ

songs for the newborn   dead king   a flower

we are not who you think we are

"We are not who you think we are" is an anomaly. Very rarely do we encounter direct address in the poems. Here, this line seems to suggest a certain relation with the spiritworld. The gods appear alien to man, who is fearful because he does not understand the laws of the invisible. In the mirror, he is confronted with an image that is foreign. Man is led down the path of intellectual enquiry and rational explanation. He seeks fixed notions of himself and the world. Thus he fails to recognize the god that resides in him.

ò

a god(s) [the nature of the god is not known]

The plural form of ò is indistinguishable from the singular. This suggests the mysterious dual nature of the gods. It is an essential characteristic.

H̦æeËÈOßÉ̆O‴Tæ»_ ƒÊlN:Kƒ˘"N §äÌ3"¶∆$äFâô/JPƒrbé[‰•ü}
ŸQÃÏd[ƒ,úSŸ…l1˜àx{Üê#bƒGƒ\N¶àoāX3ÌòÃÒ[ql2áô

an ancient city   origin   spoken of   in whispers

now plague-ridden   decline   infects the wind

sun grows dark

the blind prophet can no longer speak

"Origin" "spoken of in whispers" = the hermetic knowledge. The "ancient city" refers to a prelapsarian world, i.e. not merely "ancient" in the sense of old. "Plague-ridden decline" suggests that man has failed to realize his true nature in terms of an alchemical transformation. The "blind prophet" is man. He can no longer speak because his words are inadequate.

ECqBπ–*Ö*°Z ¨:] –=höÇ~Öfi√L2¨
√

Untranslatable. But the orientation of the signs and the signs themselves suggest a nightmare. Particularly the glyphs *Ö*°Z and höÇ.

¯ÜÉ·5púÁ¿˘N∏ÆÉè¡Ì¯:|Åü√≥@à

a god takes hold of the child's wrist

Contact. Synthesis. A god takes hold of the child/prophet's wrist. The poet here, because of the form of the glyphs, suggests a sensuality that cannot be expressed in English. The link with the god-like is a sensual, almost erotic feeling that leads to bliss.

Îáebÿĭ~ĬlĬ9Ï v˚G*f*,ÃpÓ∏óá+«5·Œ,q∏yº^
oÉ√≥ÒŸ¯|=æ
⌧?éü'HtvÑ`Ba3°Ç–B∏DxHxE$'â÷*f*"ó∏âXA<NºB%æ#…
êÙI.§Híê¥ìtÑtûtèÙäL&kì…dy'πë|ë¸ò¸VÇ"a·%¡ñÿ(Q%—
.1(ÒB/%È$πV2G≤\Ú8‰
…i)º î∂î ãSjÉTï')aYiä¥¥üt≤t±tìÙUÈÏ¨å∂åõ

all is   darkness

king and queen   dissolve   the city of water

child holds the plume

writes in the book   a song   the double flame

hand under water   eyes behind eyes

Absolute darkness is the prelude to total synthesis during the alchemical process. We imagine here the rest of the poem is a description of the final conjunction of the elements. "King and queen" are united and "dissolve" = male and female merge. Self is no longer double. "The city of water = world is fluid, not hard. The "child holds the plume" = a tool for writing. He writes the book of nature. "Hands under water" and "eyes behind eyes" signify "as above so below." "Eye" here refers to the bright sun. "Hands under water" is a strange colloquial phrase meaning "one has descended into the underworld," which was thought to be located deep under the sea.

[&_Ê∞ÃEô1 B—†∏PXî-îz % 8C'°zQE'o"YŸe≤°≤Y≤U≤gdGhMōÊEK¢ī–N–ÜhÔó(/qZ¬Y≤cIÀí¡%srärérπBπVπ;rÔÂÈÚnÚâÚªÂ;‰) †Ù2

plague and famine   after battle   dead king

the child seeks shelter   hand inside the sun   clasps the knife

for revenge

Here the poet seems to be describing an historical event. Plague and famine have overcome the besieged city. The king is dead. The barbarians have taken possession of the city. The child/prophet "seeks shelter" and "revenge." He puts his "hand inside the sun" and "clasps the knife." This suggests a cleansing in preparation for a counterattack. The resurrection of hermetic knowledge. It may also mean that the child is reaching into the "hermetic current" in order to access secret knowledge. The word for revenge is †Ù2. Here it has the primary sense of "correction," as in a "corrective" to some aberration in the order of the magical universe. It may also suggest defense against a magickal act.

\RòV§/*≤
O(fiWÇïÙïi÷) ã°ØµO´ VÍSöUVQˆPNUfiØ|QyZÖ¶,í†R¶rVeJï¢jØ U-S=ß˙å.
Kw¢'—+Ë=Ù5%5O5°Z≠Zø/°∫ézàzûz´#
ÇC#V£L£[cFSU"W3W≥YÛæ^ ã°ØµO´, WkN[G;L{õvá^§éúéóNéN≥ŒC]≤
ÆÉnönùÓm=åC/QÔÄfiM}XflB?^øJ˘Ûl`i¿58`0∞Ω´z)oi›"aCí°ìaÜa≥·Õ»«(œ√Ë
Ö±¶qÑÒn„^„O&≠l&ı&LeLWòÊôvô¸j¶o∆2´2ªmN6w7flhfii¸rôı2Œ≤ÉÀÓZ-
P,|-∂Yt[|¥¥≤‰o[∂XNYiZE[U[

corroded book   **evil erupts**   **none left**   **all dead**

infected water   **queen weeping**   **king sick**

prophetic books   **put down**   **the earth opens up**

vomit   **words**

A rather bizarre one. It is concerned with language itself. This suggests it is a much later poem. The prophetic books are "corroded" = ignored. The rest of the poem has a double hermetic/actual meaning. Then we come to "the earth opens up...vomit[s] words." My feeling is that something has been lost or corrupted in the language. A guess would be that the earth retaliates for a violation of the natural order of things, in which case the words would be equivalent to curses or verbal banishments of the present "evil." A unique word, "evil," ã°ØμO´, that is qualitative. This suggests that it may be a late edition or a corruption. Formerly, there was no word that meant "good" or, by contrast, "evil."

⊠F1„ä5//Ÿz£ıiÎw6ñ6ō6øÿ/&/6ŸN.◊YŒY^ø|ĀN›éiWk-
7bOΣèð?d?,†Ê¿tsx,·»vlpúp"sJp:ÊÙ¬ŸƒôÔ‹Ê<Áb„≤fiÂº+,Í·ZË/Ô&„‚VÈˆÿ]›
=ŒΩŸ}Δ√¬cù«yO¥ßΣÁnœa/e/ñW£◊Ā ÎWÙxìºÉº+Ωü ̄Ëº}∫|aflæ{|Æ·Z…
[Ÿ·‚º˚¯=Ú◊ÒOÛˇ>‡P4–407∞7àˋÙ&ÿ9][$¯Aànà0§;T242¥1t.
Ã5¨4ldïÒ™ı́Æá+Ñs√;#∞°
≥›VÔ]=iY9¥FgM÷ö´k÷&≠=%≈å:çé

ecstasis   sacrifice   fire

the dead king drowns   the queen turns red

watery sun   moon behind   under the earth

the child opens his eyes   sees the altar

a virgin material   knowledge of birds

orgiastic dome   in palm of child

under tongue of prophet

"Ecstasis," "sacrifice," and "fire" all suggest a ritual working. The following lines are to be read alchemically. The child opens his eyes and witnesses the altar that signifies the god-world. "Virgin material" refers to the cleansing of the body. "Knowledge of birds" is knowledge of the correspondence of the elements. It also signifies "hermetic knowledge" in general. "Orgiastic dome" suggests a grail of some sort. The child holds it in his hand but also under his tongue, which suggests prophecy. That is, the "secret way" is known to none but initiates.

tÒrp§∏/8Ê
p≤,Cπ§§fÛπqÒʃ.KènjmÕ†{r2ì8Å°?ìï»‰≥È.)…
L^6āg,,qmÈ¢"[öZ[Zöô~Q˜ʃ ̄7%ÓÌ"Ω ˉ‹3à÷ˉáÌØ¸RÍ`Āāj≥Î[Ā~:∂w˜õÊ!$E}
køÒ≈yh,yâRmåç333ç∏ñē∏†ø̂Î⌧:¸
}Ò=#ÒvøóáÓ âe ìtq›X)I)B>==ï…,–
ˇ‹ƒ˜8ØÛX»âÂ9<QDh ∏º8QªylÆÄõ¬£sy ̄â ̄0ÏOZúkë(ıü5 H›†‰oÁ>Ä¢yP‹ıfl°
ÊÉ,õ¶:±8˜ü˝Æpâ˘ëŒçˊÁLg   ˜āk,k   –Ā$»†tÅ!0V¿87∞ˉÅˋ

the snake coils   around his [?] wrist   bright sun

a god is meant   listen   to the dead   the child whispers

a jewel under his [?] tongue   the queen screams

strange dream   seek the original word

radiant talisman   for protection   from ghosts

A characteristic of the language is that it is neutral with regard to gender. There is no word for "he" or "she." "The snake coils   around his [?] wrist" suggests a communion between man and nature, acknowledging the "bright sun," the correspondence between all things. There is a "jewel" = hidden knowledge, spoken in secrecy, i.e. "under his [?] tongue." The "queen screams" is an alchemical phrase that refers to the burning of the elements. The "original word" is referred to as a "radiant talisman" for protection "from ghosts" = original word is the ur-text or logos. "Ghosts" here are forces that impel man to ignore his true will. They stand for psychological states that man must master in himself. They are the demons spoken of in all the hermetic texts.

:

This glyph is known as the portal to the invisible. It suggests in its form the handle of an invisible door.

What follows is a series of numbers that have confused scholars for years.

722 556 667 722 722 1000 722 722 667 0 0 0 0 0 500 556 444 556 444 333 500 556

278 333 556 278 833 556 500 556 556 444 389 333 556 500 722 500 500 444 0 0 0 0 0 0

0 0 0 0 1000 0 0 0 0 0 0 0 0 0 0 333 500 500 0 500 0 0 0 0 0 0 0 0 0 0 0 0 0 0 0 0

0 0 0 0 0 0 0 0 0 0 0 0 0 0 0 0 0 0 0 0 0 0 0 0 0 0 0 0 0 0 0 0 0 0 0 0 0 0 0 0

0 0 0 0 0 0 0 0 500 500 0 0 0 0 0 444 444 0 0 278 0 0 0 0 0 500 0 0 0 0 0 0 556 0

It has been argued that the series of poems does not end with the one above and that there is a large portion of the text missing. Yet the continuity of the texts discussed here would suggest the opposite and there is no evidence of significant fracture in the tablet. Scholars continue to puzzle over the sudden switch to a completely numerological language. I once believed that the numbers referred to a secret code but that has been disproven by many of the leading men and women in the field of cryptology.

Whenever I look at the series of numbers I feel a chill in my bones. Perhaps this document was written by the enemies of mankind to lure potential readers into a false and destructive belief. I work day and night, poring over books on mythology, magic, science, and religion, trying to appease my growing anxiety.

I have purchased a gun and it is on the table before me as I write. Will the day come when I am forced to use it? How can I continue to live if I discover that all these years of work have led me down a path that ends in total darkness?

William runs into David at a conference on "Androgyny and the Magickal Arts."

David is there with his new boy/girl friend.

"Can we talk?"

"Yeah, sure. Excuse me…"

William is annoyed.

"I need you to infiltrate the upper ranks of the Wild Boys. Word on the street is that Carl is looking to 'retire.' By the looks of his boys these days I don't think he'll have an easy time recruiting a replacement. Just the other day I saw a group of them strung out on heroin wandering through the streets like ghosts. The days of the "magick rides" are coming to a close. Seems the people are starting to rise up. The days of good old-fashioned anarchic magick are over. The "barbaric angel" of the prophetic books is preparing to manifest. And I assure you the Sect of the Scorpion will be ready."

"Sure. No problem. Carl trusts me. By the way, another body was found…and the people are talking about the possibility of plague."

"Nonsense my boy. Just like all that talk about an elite group that controls the planet. A fantasy to enslave the people."

Alexa keeps reading:

...because of the contradiction that, on the one hand, we started out by protesting and fighting against imperialism where, for example, we went to the streets to protest about the massacres against the Vietnamese, but now must see members of the movement, in an attempt to free prisoners with whom the people can in no way identify, hold hostage defenseless civilians who are completely uninvolved, among them women, children and the elderly.

Johnny Bellow's body was found 2 weeks later. The Black Snakes want David dead.

The Lizard is a shape-shifter. Neither man nor animal, he is a force. Throughout the centuries he has been known by many names: the Black Death, The Bubonic Plague, HIV, etc. It is he who enters the minds of kings and dictators driving them to revolution or war. It is he who spreads infectious and deadly disease throughout history. He belongs to no party and is bound to nothing except the abyss of evil that is said to dwell in the bowels of the earth.

Paul is walking on a path in the forest. There is a light rain. He looks at the printout he is holding in his hand. He reads:
…something on the radio this morning 9:27 a.m. about a plane crashing into the Twin Towers.

He knows that was written many centuries ago.

And then he comes to a sudden stop as if in shock. He looks up at the sky and thinks:
I remember reading about all the conflicting, and in some cases inflammatory, messages that circulated in the underground press after the 9/11 attacks. Those that were the most "Un-American" fascinated me. The inability of the mass media to respond to these claims led some prominent thinkers to form an independent party in order to try to make sense of this "anti-American" rage. It was shot down by the authorities and members received death threats on a daily basis.

Exterminating Angel 6

ruthless investments continue in the outside world where speculative frenzy is at a maximum   a roll of the dice   millions down on the table   the president's fist adorned with gold rings

advertising unable to stop generating false pleasures   feeding on a population whose fantasies threaten to replace reality   senators masturbate over possible gains and world domination   orgasms of superiority and hysterical arrogance

reality cluttered with illusions of a better, brighter world

accessible from your computer screen   google facebook yahoo   safe in your home   while the infrastructure is rotting near the oil pumps

and the water in some areas is undrinkable

Joey turns up the stereo and lights a big fat joint. Takes out his cock and jerks off to a woman masturbating online.

He's 21, 5'6", 120 lbs., with a boyish pockmarked face. A loner at heart. Looks like an easy target.

Look closer and you'll find 5 dead policemen in his closet. 10 human skulls in his refrigerator. 3 female fundamentalists hanging from the ceiling in his bedroom. And in the basement you'll find enough artillery to man a small army.

His rap sheet states he's killed over 300 people in cold blood. No questions asked. His motto: NO HOPE NO FEAR.

He's worked for the Black Snakes for a little over a year.

He's finished. Turns the stereo way down. Turns off the computer. Hears the phone ringing. After the 10th ring, he picks up. "Hello." "Hello Joey." "Yeah." "I've got a job for you." "Uh huh." "4 men have already turned it down. It's extremely dangerous. But I know you're the man for it." "Sure, in the name of the black serpent." "In the name of black serpent."

After his morning yoga, William fixes himself a gin and tonic and takes a seat on his throne. On the wall behind him is a large golden scorpion. He takes one sip and puts the drink down. He is relaxing and breathing slowly. In 5 minutes he enters into an astral trance.

Meanwhile David has managed to arrange a meeting with Carl. He's been standing around the corner from the head offices of the Wild Boys for 20 minutes. He holds a knife in his hand. 20 minutes turns into 30, then into 40. Suddenly, he can hear William's voice in his ear. It is as though he is standing next to him. "It's a set up. He's not coming. Get the fuck out of there."

Alexa has finished reading. She puts the documents down on the kitchen table. She paces back and forth for about 20 minutes. Then she sits down and lights a cigarette. She feels a pain in her right shoulder. A knife wound thanks to homeland security. She is thinking of Paul:

He doesn't know how much trouble he's in. He is a marked man. Carl's patience has worn thin. His respect for me won't allow him to contemplate the fact of my complicity. I know that his cancer is inoperable and it is only a matter of time before he is replaced by someone else. But I love Paul and wherever he goes I will stand by his side to the end.

Exterminating Angel 7

principia misogynistic noble profile the masses don't feel pain rictus horribile degenerate incest Lucia in the Valkyries of Wagner ice swan pounds of caviar masonic hermeticism

angel or beast out of darkness

Exterminating Angel 8

fear and desperation spawn a belief in false myth and fetishes, Kabbalah, chicken feet and washable rubber virgin brutal rituals of human sacrifice we've had the habits and proclivities and tastes of imperialists, so we've colonized what we've thought of as the 'strong' sounds in nature, while leaving a whole spectrum unnoticed

the tears of the gentle Fascist have spoken…………………………………………..

FACE TO FACE WITH DEATH

The Terminal Game

In Homer's *Iliad*, Ajax says, *O Father Zeus, deliver the sons of the Achaeans from this great darkness. Clear the air and enable our eyes to see.*

About this passage, Paul writes:

Our very ability to "see clearly" is contingent upon a belief in some higher authority as embodied in the ideas of one man or a collective who leads the flock and is in possession of the truth. And yet the self is fragile and inclined to shatter into a million pieces when the pressure of belief is great enough. And then the psychotic personality emerges.

On the margin of his notebook he copies two lines from the *Iliad*:

Zeus snaps and breaks the carefully wrought string of Teucer's bow, preventing him from wounding a Trojan.

Phoebus Apollo shrouded in mist.

Paul is almost finished with the book on terrorism. He firmly believes that whatever means are used to alter the direction of society are subject to the laws of revolution and herein lies the problem of actualizing them. His closing words: *A murderer abandons the moral value system. The revolutionary surmounts it. That means the moral righteousness of the revolutionary, which can easily lead to an arrogant presumptuousness, at the same time provides the basis to overcome the qualms that a leftist group has with regard to killing someone. We judge the enemy morally, condemn them, and based on this moral judgment we recognize them as evil. That means we believe that personal guilt plays a role in this. It is necessary for our liberation, and therefore it is also justified to destroy this evil, even if in human form. But so little of this moral indignation has been turned into effective political action in the Imperial City. Now, it is just a matter of violence, retribution for wrong. The mob rules. Our higher consciousness has only facilitated more elaborate and intricate methods of destruction.*

Carl is rushed to the hospital. Only a few of his closest friends accompany him.

But word leaked out onto the street about Carl.
William is all ears.

He was waiting for this day all his life. Now is the time to move in. He sends a message to his inner circle to prepare them for the rite of the Black Sun.

Joey gets impatient when there's a delay. He looks at his watch. 5:34 p.m. He received a tip about a bar called the Iron Hole where David could be found almost daily around 5 p.m. He was told he was coming here today. He had decided he would use a different method to deal with the situation. He realized that David was a crazy motherfucker. No crazier than I am, he thought. He uses a special brand of witchcraft.

With a razor he makes a small cut on his arm. Smears the blood on his fingers.
Improvises a magick circle. With blood on the middle finger of his left hand he draws her sign in the air. Intones silently her name: *Liiiiiiiliiiiiiith, Liiiiiiiiliiiiith, come forth and bring thy cup of abominations that I shall drink the last drop of.*

David enters the Iron Hole and orders a beer. The woman next to him catches his eye. Her hair is fiery scarlet and her eyes are as black as the deepest abyss. He sees the ring on her middle finger. The sign of Set. She radiates a dark sexual energy. He is vaguely nauseous from the overwhelming electric charge flooding his body. But at the same time he feels a hand in his pants and this turns him on.

She said her name was Desirée.

After speaking to her for an hour he excuses himself. He goes to the bathroom, enters a stall and locks it. He says to himself, "I knew it." He improvises one of the most dangerous rituals in the canon, reserved only for the most extreme cases: the rite of Orpheus. It is concerned with travel into the past. This act breaks every magickal law and potentially causes a permanent rupture in time and space. David knows this but he also knows that he is a marked man.

He feels like he is moving in water. The air is elastic. Then almost unbearable pressure on his chest. The colors of the spectrum bend. Then absolute darkness. Screams. Then silence. Voices. The sound of laughter. All this time he feels like he is moving very fast. Then the darkness slowly disappears.

He sees a man cutting himself. He is performing some kind of ritual. Then red smoke from which a woman emerges.

"It's her. I fucking knew it."

He turns away from her in disgust.

But he is unable to move. It is as though the air around him had congealed and acted like a glass door through which he could see hooded figures wavering in front of him, barely visible. These are the Guardians of the Gate. They ensure that no one trespasses the Law of Time.

David is trapped in an eternally recurring moment, a thin slice of *negative time* opened up between the present and the past.

David's physical body was found 3 hours later on a bed in a hotel room. He had been strangled.

Sun aligns with Moon.

An hour later the sun is eclipsed.

A five-mile radius around the Wild Boys' headquarters is plunged into darkness.

William's eyes are closed. He is breathing steadily. His thoughts are all of fire.

In a remote outpost far from the Imperial City, Carl dies, quietly. His work on the alien language follows him to the grave. At peace and in good conscience this very night he had made contact with the entity and implored it to destroy all the documents. Which was promptly done.

Joey is arrested by the special police on charges of the violation of magickal law. He is put in a cell. 15 minutes later he vanishes.

A prison guard is rushed to the hospital. There is a gash the size of a small fist beneath his ribcage.

A helix of fire engulfs the Wild Boys' headquarters.

In the absence of Carl, the Wild Boys panic. He had taken certain secrets that might have saved them to his grave.

In the morning, there is a mound of dirt where the Wild Boys' headquarters formerly stood. A wisp of smoke lingers in the air for a second and is gone.

The remaining Wild Boys begin the long migration toward the wastelands. They are no longer safe here.

William opens his eyes. He takes a deep breath. He is relieved.

A minute later he hears a knock. He turns his head and looks at the door. "Who could this be," he thinks to himself.

   "Who is it?"
   "It's me."
   "Ahhh, Dorian, come in."

10 hours later William is found dead on the floor next to his throne. There is a dark patch over his genitals and his rotted penis gives off a putrid stench. By this time ¾ of his body is covered in large black sores.

During questioning the following day, Dorian tells the secret police that he had been to William's apartment about a week ago only to find no one home. He hadn't been there since.

Astrologers and doctors convene in an undisclosed location to discuss the plague.
The dead are multiplying. The people are afraid.

On a wall of the Justice Building someone has spray-painted:

THIS DISEASE IS VIOLENT, STORMY, RAPID, MONSTROUS, TERRIFYING, CONTAGIOUS, HORRIBLE, A WILD BEAST, FIERCE AND VERY CRUEL, A DEADLY ENEMY OF MAN.

Absolute terror grips the people. The message causes widespread panic throughout the Imperial City. People begin to make preparations to leave. But to go where? It is the only world they know. There is no outside. They do not know what they will find as they journey beyond the city limits. It is said that vast walls surround the city, beyond which there is nothing but a sprawling wasteland.

An astrologer observed the conjunction of Saturn, Jupiter, and Mars.

Top Secret: Observations On The Advancing Plague

INVASION STAGE 1: Sudden explosive onset of hyper-acute infection, prostration, diarrhea, and vomiting.

INVASION STAGE 2^9: The patient complains of a rasping cough. One notes a rapid, short, and superficial respiration, and production of a blood-tinged cough.

ADVANCED STAGE: Evolution toward septic shock and coma. Intravascular clotting, acute respiratory distress, and heart failure are terminal complications. By this time the body is covered with dark, bulbous sores.

---

9 This second stage could vary anywhere from 2 days to minutes after the initial invasion.

Alexa wakes from a nightmare. In it, she was bound by her hands and legs and left in a dark cave where her flesh was being torn apart by rats.

The Lizard is working overtime.

Alexa and Paul decide to leave. Neither believes the various advertisements that tell them not to worry and that everything will be okay.

They begin the long migration to the wastelands. At 150 miles per hour.

Joey adds another cop to his collection.

He thinks, "With David dead, and Carl dead, and William dead the whole fucking charade is falling apart. Got to get my Mojo workin'. Now's the time to move in. Long live Anarchy."

He lies down in bed. Turns the stereo up. Joe Clay's rockabilly classic "Sixteen Chicks" comes strolling out of the speakers.

Meanwhile, the body count rises. The streets are desolate. Not a sound can be heard.

The sickly wind carries infection on its hunched back.

They arrive at an outpost in the wastelands. Once inside, Alexa puts her arms around Paul's neck and holds tight. As if for dear life. He feels her body trembling.

Joey scratches his balls. Gets up to take a piss. Walking to the bathroom he thinks, "I hope that bitch didn't give me the clap. Ah, but she was a good one." He leans over the toilet and unzips.

"WHAT THE FUCK!"

5 hours later, the Catman announces another rockabilly killer:

"OK here's one for you kiddies by a Mr. Theodore Harris, one time disc jockey who wrote songs for Hank Snow's Silver Star Publishing and recorded a couple of singles for Columbia in far off 1960 E.V. Should be better known, I reckon. It's a little gem called 'Just Thought I'd Set You Straight.'"

Joey's speakers are starting to crackle. Probably blown.

Exterminating Angel
Final Virus Transmission

replicating pestilence   the light gone out long ago   continual rotten weather   a sudden rupture in the social fabric   spreads confusion and suicide on a large scale

of the millions who journeyed to the wasteland   less than a hundred survived

some recall the strength of the body under duress   the warrior culture   perhaps they invoke an earlier time   a golden age etc. forget it

there is no vaccine for the illness gripping this tired, bedridden city   by now it's almost completely engulfed by the plague

Here in the wasteland the Wild Boys are at home. They are armed. Paul continues to work on his book, taking notes on what he knows of the plague. Alexa, as Babalon, assumes the leadership of the Wild Boys.

One month later.

In the distance they see movement.

"Who or what is that"?

"It appears to be a man walking towards us."

"Out here in this wasteland, alone?"

The man is moving at an average pace. Not quickly. Not slowly.
He appears neither aggressive nor passive.
There is something ageless about him.
A strange darkness in his eyes.
A vague smile on his lips.
He is not without a sense of humor.

No one is left. Dead bodies are scattered among the wastes. Alexa, Paul, and the Wild Boys are just names in an unwritten history.

A page from the book Paul was writing is picked up by a breeze and tossed into a heap of broken television sets, Atari games, books on Fortran programming, land line telephones, old clothes, used condoms, Joey's speakers, telephone books, discarded newspapers, chewing gum, cheap romance novels, faded photographs, children's toys.

The junk of the past.

The stranger continues walking in the opposite direction. His work is done for now.

PETER VALENTE is the author of 7 books, the most recent of which is a translation of Nanni Balestrini's *Blackout* (Commune Editions, 2017), and a couple of chapbooks. Forthcoming is his collaboration with Kevin Killian, "Ekstasis" (Blazevox, 2017). His poems, essays, and photographs have appeared in journals such as *Mirage #4/Periodical, First Intensity, Aufgabe, Talisman, Oyster Boy Review*, and *spoKe*. In 2019, City Lights will publish his co-translation of 33 of Artaud's late letters (1945-1947) with an introduction by Stephen Barber. Presently, he is at work on a book for Semiotext(e). In addition, he has made 60 short films, 24 of which were shown at Anthology Film Archives.

Made in the USA
Middletown, DE
12 August 2019